CAMANCHACA

CAMANCHACA

Diego Zúñiga

Translated by Megan McDowell

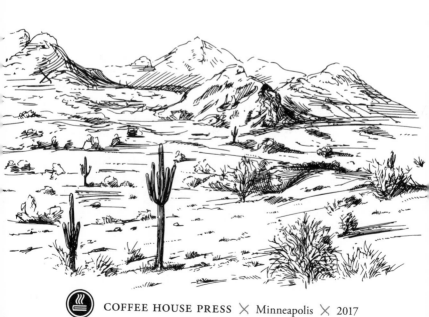

COFFEE HOUSE PRESS ✕ Minneapolis ✕ 2017

Cover images: desert photo © gkuna/iStock; lined paper © Retrovizor/iStock; antique map of South America © Mastamak/iStock; desert drawing © Canicula/Shutterstock; teeth diagram © brovarky/fotolia

Coffee House Press books are available to the trade through our primary distributor, Consortium Book Sales & Distribution, cbsd.com or (800) 283-3572. For personal orders, catalogs, or other information, write to info@coffeehousepress.org.

Coffee House Press is a nonprofit literary publishing house. Support from private foundations, corporate giving programs, government programs, and generous individuals helps make the publication of our books possible. We gratefully acknowledge their support in detail in the back of this book.

Library of Congress Cataloging-in-Publication Data
Names: Zúñiga, Diego, 1987– author. | McDowell, Megan, translator.
Title: Camanchaca / Diego Zúñiga ; translated by Megan McDowell.
Other titles: Camanchaca. English
Description: Minneapolis : Coffee House Press, 2017. | Originally published in Spanish by Random House Mondadori (Santiago de Chile, Chile, 2012).
Identifiers: LCCN 2016027858 | ISBN 9781566894609 (paperback)
Subjects: LCSH: Mothers and sons—Fiction. | Absentee fathers—Fiction. | Broken homes—Fiction. | Family secrets—Fiction. | Grief—Fiction. | Chile—Fiction. | Psychological fiction. | Domestic fiction. | BISAC: FICTION / Literary. | FICTION / Psychological. | FICTION / Family Life.
Classification: LCC PQ8098.436.U55 C3613 2017 | DDC 863/.7—dc23
LC record available at https://lccn.loc.gov/2016027858

Printed in the United States of America
23 22 21 20 19 18 17 16   1 2 3 4 5 6 7 8

To Lorena, for all the reasons.

CAMANCHACA

My father's first car was a 1971 Ford Fairlane, which my grandfather gave him when he turned fifteen.

His second was a 1985 Honda Accord, lead gray.

His third was a 1990 BMW 850i, navy blue, which he killed my Uncle Neno with.

His fourth is a Ford Ranger, smoke colored, which we are driving across the Atacama Desert.

My parents separated when I was four years old. I'm twenty now. I live with my mother in Santiago. My father stayed in Iquique with his new family. Sometimes we see each other when he travels for business. He takes me clothes shopping or asks me to go pick up some boxes with him and his new wife. I get into his truck, put my headphones on, turn on my music, and go with him.

Now he tells me we have to go to Tacna or I could lose my teeth—he knows a dentist who will help me save them. He explains this, and his ten-year-old son, who is riding in the backseat of the truck, bursts out laughing and says something I don't catch. He laughs, and my father's wife tells him, "Eddie, be quiet," but he doesn't stop laughing.

My mother lost all her teeth. She had to get a dental plate. Sometimes she goes to the kitchen and opens the drawer where she keeps the special cream, then she turns her back to me and adjusts the upper denture. I look at her face reflected in the kitchen window and say nothing. Then she turns back around, and there she is, her upper teeth in place. She doesn't use the bottom part. She says it hurts, and she can't sleep when she wears it.

My father's wife is named Nancy. My mother says Nancy used to walk Thompson Street, and that's where she met my father. Sometimes I get the urge to ask her. Right now, for example, as she's offering me a cup of soda, I look at her in the rearview mirror and think about asking her if it's true she worked Thompson Street. I look at her. She smiles at me. She flashes me her perfect smile, and I shake my head no. Then I put on my headphones and turn my eyes toward the highway.

Before we left for the trip, my mother gave me a list of things to buy: jacket, pants, tennis shoes, shirts, underwear, and socks. She told me to insist that my father buy me brand-name things so they'd last all year. She emphasized that part. And when I called her from Coquimbo, where we were spending the night, she reminded me again to tell him he had to buy me those things. And I said o.k., picturing myself at the Iquique mall buying whatever I could find that fit, asking my father if I could have this hoodie, if I could have that shirt, and then hearing no, too expensive, pick something else. And me going into the dressing room and trying to fit into the sale shirts, figuring if I lost a few pounds when I got back to Santiago, I might be able to button those two-for-one pants.

My father's son is named Elías. That's how my grandmother introduced him to me, even though everyone calls him Eddie. He was born when I was ten years old. My mother says he's not my father's son, that the woman had an affair with another man. That's what she heard, and she believes it because the kid doesn't look anything like my father, my mother says, the kid only looks like the woman. And I look in the side mirror while he's playing some kind of Game Boy my father gave him for Christmas, and I think yes, it's true, he doesn't look much like my dad.

My mother hasn't worked since the day we arrived in Santiago. She stopped going out altogether, except when we do the grocery shopping the first week of each month. She always asks me to go with her. My grandfather sends her money, we go to the supermarket, and she buys food for the month. She also buys hair dye, but she never knows which one looks best on her, so she asks for my opinion. I look at the boxes, and I don't understand the difference between an ash blond and a matte blond. Still, I look at the woman on each box and then at my mother, and I give my opinion. Sometimes she takes my advice, but usually she doesn't, and then she leaves the hair dye aisle and goes on with the month's shopping.

My father says we're close to Antofagasta. He explains that one must respect the desert and the highway, that not just anyone can drive there. I nod, taking my headphones off. I turn my head to look at him, and he says that someday he'll teach me to drive, there's nothing to it. And I nod again. And then he puts his right hand on my thigh and says that I should lose a little weight, that if I don't lose weight something could happen to me. And I nod and put my headphones back on.

My mother and I used to play a game where we told stories before bed. We'd turn off the TV, and we had to make them up in the dark. We just started doing it, it wasn't planned, but we really enjoyed those moments. We would laugh in total darkness, in that double bed my grandfather had given us. When we came to Santiago, we decided we would sleep together. Although really, it was my mother who made the decision. She told me there was no money for gas, we couldn't have a heater, and it would be best for us to sleep in the same bed, like when I was a kid and we still lived in Iquique. Of course I didn't question it. I just grabbed a few things and moved into her room, our room.

My father beats his fingers on the steering wheel as if he's playing the drums. The woman and her son are sleeping, but he doesn't care. I turn down the volume on my MP3 player. He goes on pounding the wheel to the rhythm of drums and a guitar. It's Pat Metheny. He looks at me, a smile on his face. I take off my headphones. He's still smiling. He asks if I know this music. I nod. He drums harder on the steering wheel. When the song is over, he tells me about the time he saw Pat Metheny live at the Chile Stadium, when he took Nancy. Then he tells me that if Metheny ever comes back, he'll take me. I don't say anything. I look out the right-hand window. A man, walking in the desert. I watch him for a few seconds before we leave him behind and he vanishes among the hills. I see him and I imagine being him, crossing the desert, getting lost. An empampado: swallowed by the pampa. I like that word. Empampado. We leave him behind. Another Pat Metheny song comes on, and my father again starts drumming on the wheel.

It was one of those nights, in total darkness, when my mother told me what happened to my Uncle Neno. She said there was a lot I didn't know, that it hadn't been her idea to lie to me, but she'd made an agreement with my grandparents. And she told the story. In complete detail. Full of silences. A few days after that, we'd never mention Uncle Neno again. A few days after that, there'd be another story nobody would want to tell.

We get out at a gas station. My father buys a couple of sodas and something to eat. I stay next to the truck, watching the woman and her son flip through some magazines while they wait for my father. I think about my last trip to Iquique. My grandmother dead. Her eyes closed and a thread of blood running from her mouth, a thread that appeared just before they closed the coffin. Then, the cemetery. They buried her with my Uncle Neno. I think that morning they had to compact my uncle's remains so she would fit in the same niche. My father didn't want to see him. My grandfather had to go instead. He said my uncle's body was mummified. My father said nothing.

The next day I didn't go to class. I don't think it was because of the story about my uncle; I just didn't feel like getting up. I was studying journalism, and I wanted to work in radio. I wanted to have a show about soccer or an interview show. My mother, on the other hand, wanted only for me to study law. She insisted I'd be lost if I studied journalism, I wouldn't have a future, that radio was crap. That's what she said. But that was my dream: some big headphones, the studio, interviewing athletes or hosting a news show. Finally I applied, and I got in. I told my father, and he congratulated me. When I told him about the enrollment fee, he said he didn't have any money. He couldn't pay the monthly tuition either. I had to apply for scholarships. Luckily, I got all of them.

"We'll take the route through the desert," says my father. "It'll take a couple more hours, but we'll get there all right," he says, and I'm left thinking about the beaches we won't see. We pass the turnoff that would have taken us to Antofagasta, and we head deeper into the desert: the coastal route is no longer an option. I've never gone to Iquique through the desert. The sun is starting to go down. My dad's son is paging through the video game magazine he just bought. The woman is looking out the window. My father puts on another Pat Metheny album.

The university also gave me a coupon book with vouchers for food. There weren't many, and I spent them all, without fail, the first week of every month. Sometimes I'd take my mother out for Chinese and pay the bill with vouchers. Otherwise I used them up myself. I'd go to classes, then at lunchtime I'd walk around downtown to see which places would accept the vouchers. One day I made a list of all the restaurants where I could use them. And I started to visit them, in Providencia, downtown, around Central Station. The action never varied much: I'd go in, sit down at an isolated table, and eat. And the vouchers never lasted past the first week of the month.

I imagine the deserted beaches. The sun beginning to set. The red ocean. The orange sky. Those places I'd gone with my family before I had a memory. Before the accident. The images don't exist outside of a few faded photos. But that's how they described it to me. The deserted beaches and my family, camping out for a couple of weeks. My father, my mother, my grandparents, and my Uncle Neno.

I also got a cash stipend. Fifteen thousand pesos a month. Sometimes I would save up for two or three months to buy clothes so I wouldn't need so many things when I went to Iquique. Once, I saved up money to buy a microphone and a tape recorder. And I started recording my voice at night, before I joined my mother in bed. I wanted to be like those ESPN commentators who did the Champions League when I was little and still living in Iquique. Like the one who reported on the final between Manchester United and Bayern Munich at the Camp Nou stadium. Supposedly he was Chilean, but his accent sounded neutral to me. And at night I used to practice that accent, trying to come up with nicknames for every Chilean player. And I'd remember that final match, that period in Iquique when my mother was working and I spent the days alone, watching the 1999 Champions League games.

The color of the sky: orange, maybe purple at times. The desert: blue, as if a blanket were covering it. There is nothing. My father is listening to another CD, a group I don't know. In the back, the woman and her son are talking in low voices. The desert looks as if it were going to sleep, tucked in under a blue blanket. And in the distance, a village. Some houses. Chacabuco. There's a man at the entrance to the town. He's drinking something from a cup while he watches the cars pass on the highway. Or that's the impression I get, at least. My dad tells me he must be crazy. The town is deserted. There are no lights; there is nothing and no one. Just the man at the entrance and the houses that blend in with the desert. My dad says it again, but I don't reply. I have my headphones on. He says the man hears voices, or that's what they say; his story is well known. I don't take my eyes off the desert. We leave the man behind. My father starts to tell me the story, but I'd rather not listen. And I imagine the man drinking the last sip from his cup and going to sleep in a house lit by a couple of candles. He waits for them to burn out, closes his eyes, and sleeps. "Surrounded by whispers," says my father. "The nightmares and shouts and whispers of all those people," he says, and I close my eyes while night falls in the desert.

Once, I got to watch that final between Manchester and Bayern again. And what I did was turn the volume down and start announcing the game. I tried to forget how it ended, though that was impossible. I related the first half calmly, until Bayern went confidently into halftime, ahead by one goal. The second half, as the Chilean announcer would say a few minutes later, was not for the faint of heart. When Lothar Matthäus was subbed out in the eightieth minute, I stood up and started clapping. Just then my mother came into my room and saw me there, in front of the TV with the microphone and recorder, giving a standing ovation. I motioned for her to leave, and she did. Finally, at minute ninety-one, the story began to change. A corner and a goal by Teddy Sheringham. I yelled so loudly my mother came back into the room and stood there watching the scene: I was shouting, trying to articulate a coherent, stirring story. I was on the verge of tears. And then came the end, a minute later, when Ole Gunnar Solskjær, the baby-faced killer, the greatest replacement of all time, blocked a ball in the box and brought glory to Manchester, to England, an entire country watching its team turn that scoreboard around. An epic story, a match for the ages, damn good soccer.

The final stretch. Alto Hospicio. Lights in the darkness. Streets lit with low-intensity bulbs. Two women walking along the edge of the highway. One of them puts out her thumb. My father drives in silence while his family sleeps. When I left Iquique, Alto Hospicio didn't yet exist. There were five houses in the middle of the desert, along with a couple of illegal garbage dumps. Now it's a city, I think to myself, a city with lit streets. My father turns on the radio and manages to pick up an Iquique station. A man is talking about a fire. There are no fatalities, only injured people, the announcer says as we start to descend from the hills into Iquique. Lights that move away from a black stain: the ocean. A few dots scattered in the black stain, around the port. The soccer stadium with its field lit up. The yellow city, us going down, the family awake now, and the man on the radio who leaves us with a song by Amerikan Sound. My father turns off the radio and tells me we've arrived. I nod, thinking I should call my mother; I don't want to.

I also practiced doing an interview program. I asked the questions, and I answered them too. The idea was to put myself to the test, so I tried to give complex responses that might make me draw a blank. I wanted to gauge my ability to react and improvise, the way my professors had recently taught me. It lasted a couple of episodes, then my mother came in and asked me why I didn't interview her.

That was the start of the interviews. That was the start of the stories.

We're in Iquique. We go to my grandpa's house. That's where I'll be staying for summer vacation. It's strange to go inside and not find my grandmother there. The house seems bigger. It smells musty, unaired. My grandpa comes out to greet me. He's wearing an apron. Then he looks me over and tells me I'm very fat, that I need to take care of myself. I don't say anything. I go to the master bedroom. The portrait of my grandmother is still hanging on the wall. I leave and go sit down at the table. My father is telling my grandpa about our trip to Buenos Aires, the wonders of the Buenos Aires trip. Nancy is sitting next to him with her son. They smile while my dad tells my grandpa that he bought me some books. He looks at me, and I smile back and tell him yes, he bought me three books. Then my dad leaves, and I'm alone with my grandpa, in silence.

The interviews happened at night. Sometimes we let Coka come in and keep us company. We'd sit in the living room: two glasses of water, an ashtray, her cigarettes and lighter, the recorder, the microphone, and a radio. It was a classic format: three fifteen-minute blocks with a couple of songs in between. We decided to start with childhood. My mom was obsessed with childhood, her childhood. And there was one image she couldn't forget: the day her mother left. She remembered her mother hastily packing a suitcase, and her sister crying, pleading with her not to go, not to abandon them. And my grandmother, totally silent as she threw clothes into the suitcase.

"Why was she in such a rush?"

"I don't know," replied my mom, and she lit a cigarette. "I guess she thought my dad would be back soon. And I was worried about that, too, about my dad finding her in the house before she left."

"And what did your dad say when he came back and she wasn't there?"

"I don't think he said anything. He just shut himself in his room and started to cry."

The trip to Buenos Aires was for business. My dad invited me right after what happened with my mom, and I accepted immediately. We went for five days. He promised he'd buy me some books, since they were cheaper in Argentina. And the last day of the trip came, we were exhausted, and I still had no books. He wanted to stay lying down in the room, but I told him that was nuts, we had to make the most of our time. Finally, we went to Calle Florida; him window-shopping with the woman and her son, me running, going into all the bookstores and hunting for a book I wanted to buy. I'd had a list in mind, but I forgot it. By then it didn't matter. They strolled, and I dashed into bookstores and lost sight of them. It was getting dark, and the stores were starting to close. And then one last bookstore at the end of Florida, while my dad was back at a mall, and I found three novels I wanted, they weren't on the list but they were ones I wanted. And then searching for him and telling him we have to run, the bookstore's closing in five minutes. The two of us running, and the sales clerk who handed me the books, and my dad, who paid and asked me if I was happy now, and I said nothing, I was looking at the novels and thinking about how we had to go back. And he was slapping me on the back and asking if I could use those books in school. "Yes, Dad, thanks. Yes, Dad," I was saying, and he was smiling and asking to hold the books, and looking at them, touching them. He took one by its front and back covers and turned it over—it looked like a bird in flight—and he was telling me it was really sturdy, you could tell it was a quality book, and I was quiet, looking at the open book and at him shaking it and talking about quality, and I said nothing, thinking about how the next day, we had to go back to Chile.

In one of the interviews, she told me it's better not to remember anything.

The image: walking down Calle Florida, my dad slapping me on the back and telling me how lucky I am, how not all sons have a father like him. That's what he told me, with his smile, and I looked at him and nodded, and he was slapping my back and telling me I'd never forget that trip to Buenos Aires, that it would be something I could tell my kids about, an important event in my life. And I looked at him and he was smiling, slapping my back and smiling at me.

One day she decided we would switch places. She wanted me to answer the questions and choose the songs. And she asked me about my childhood. I gave vague replies. For a second I thought about telling her I had no childhood memories, that I had a terrible memory, but I knew that if I did, the interview would only last a few minutes. So I called a few moments to mind: the day my parents separated, the baseball games in Morro, the afternoons alone in the apartment while I waited for her to come home, the day my dad took me to the beach and told me I was lucky to be an only child.

My grandfather asks about my mother. I tell him everything's fine. Then he tells me to go up and see which room I want to stay in. Before my mom and I went to live in Santiago, we spent a few months in this house. Now it's not a house anymore; it's a boarding house with a bunch of rooms I've never seen. I go up the stairs. My grandfather watches me from below, leaning on his cane. I go up. It's a different place now. There's a long hallway, some chairs in one corner and a TV installed in another. It looks like the black apparatus holding it up could fall any second. The TV is off, and the chairs are a bit jumbled. The living room doesn't exist anymore, nor does the kitchen or anything else. There are only bedrooms. Many bedrooms opening to either side of the hallway. The doors are all closed. They're numbered. I don't know which one to open. My grandfather shouts something I can't make out. I keep walking. Now there are no more rooms, just the hallway that leads outside and to the bathrooms. I follow it out. I can see down into my grandfather's yard, and I can see the clock up on the hill. It says it's 11:07 p.m. There are the roofs of the other houses. I think this is the only building on the block with two floors. I can see the roofs and the yards. The sky is dark. I can't hear my grandfather's voice anymore. Off of this outdoor walkway there are two bathrooms and also a bedroom. I open the door. There's no one inside. I sit on the bed. Then I lie down. Close my eyes.

"What do you remember about the day we separated?" she asked me. Her tone was strange, as if she were trying to make her voice huskier.

"I don't know," I answered. "To tell the truth, I never really understood why you separated."

"But you must remember something," she insisted.

"Maybe something," I said, and then I was silent.

But I did. I had an image: My cousin and I were playing hide-and-seek. We were at my grandfather's house. She was counting, and I went outside to hide behind some bushes. She found me and started to chase me, and I ran to the house. I dashed inside and closed the door without looking behind me. She had her hand in the doorjamb. She started to scream. My dad and my mom appeared. I think one of them tried to hit me. Then came the yelling. Then my mom and I left that house.

I open my eyes. The room is dark. I turn on a lamp. My bag and jacket are at the foot of the bed. I taste blood on my teeth. I lick them, then get up and open the door. Downstairs the yard is dark. I can't see the clock on the hill anymore. I don't know if there's fog or if it just turns off at a certain time. I don't remember that detail. My grandfather must be asleep, I think, and I move along the hallway and go down into the house. The lights are out in all the rooms. Just before the stairs, there are some men watching a tennis match on TV. I say hello, but they don't reply; they go on watching the tennis game and drinking from beer cans. I leave them there and stand still on the stairs. A black spiral staircase. I'm positive I fell down it once when I was a kid. I know I rolled and I probably started bawling. Now I go down slowly and look at each step, and I wonder how my mother was able to go down these stairs without falling. I think about my mother, fat and clumsy, barely able to make it downstairs, maybe taking five or ten minutes. I think how at some point, a man saw her from the street and stood still, watching how she went down each step, how she never let go of the railing. And now I'm going down, too, without letting go of the railing.

"What makes you think that's why we separated?" asked my mother. "Why are you so sure we separated because of what happened that day?"

"I didn't say I was sure," I replied. "I just remember that after that day, you weren't together."

"And what happened after you slammed your cousin's fingers in the door?"

"I didn't slam her fingers in the door. It was an accident."

"But what else do you remember?"

"I remember my cousin screaming, you and Dad shouting, and that my grandparents weren't there. I never figured out why they didn't come. I know that I started to cry, and I went up the spiral staircase and locked myself in my room. I was four years old. Or maybe five. Then my cousin came upstairs, and she asked me if what my mom had said was true. If it was true I was leaving the house. I guess I said no. Or maybe I just went on crying. The image gets blurry after that. I don't know what comes next. But I never saw my cousin again."

I reach the ground floor. I open the door, and my grandpa is sitting at his desk, reading. He looks up and asks me what's on my teeth. I tell him they bleed when I sleep. "You have to take care of yourself, boy," he tells me. "You could lose them all, and then you really won't find work anywhere." I nod. "You read the Bible, right?" he asks me, and I nod again. "That's good, son, it's good that you read the Bible," he tells me, "because the end of the world is coming, and Jehovah, who art in heaven, needs learned men, men who understand his word. Great Babylon is strong, very strong. Did you know that, son? But look, things are going to change, and we'll meet your grandmother again. She'll be resurrected and we'll all be happy," says my grandpa.

"And will my uncle be resurrected too?" I ask, and my grandpa looks at me and shakes his head no. Then he lowers his gaze and goes on turning the Bible's pages.

After that interview I told her I'd rather keep asking the questions myself, that I preferred her answers, her stories. She said that was fine and we went on, every night, with the same ritual. Coka was our audience. She hadn't gotten sick yet; she could still walk o.k. and her bark was strong. The interviews continued. She talked about her mom, who never came home again; she talked about her dad, who was a womanizer; she talked about her siblings, scattered throughout Chile. People I had never met. People lost in little towns at the northern and southern ends of the country. I especially liked the story of one brother. He got married very young, had three kids, then disappeared along the highway between two towns in the south of Chile; I don't remember their names. But he disappeared. According to my mom, the UFOs took him. That's the story this uncle told. Although sometimes my mom changed her version and said he was arrested by the military. That they tortured him, thinking he belonged to some subversive group, and that once they realized he couldn't give them anything, they dumped him in the middle of a forest and he survived, who knows how. But the important thing was this: after being gone for twenty years, my uncle returned. My cousins, whom I've never met, didn't recognize him. His wife didn't either. I only know that they were together for a while and then he told them he had another family. He told them he'd married a girl ten years younger than him. Those were his words. The next day his first wife shot herself. They say he saw the body lying in the yard, grabbed his things, and took off.

"Are you and your mother going to come back some-day?" asks my grandpa while he puts the Bible into an old briefcase.

"I don't think so," I say. I'm really not sure, but I answer quickly, as if it were something I'd memorized. It's the never-ending argument. I know my grandpa will start talking now about why we left Iquique like that, so rashly, and I won't really know what to tell him. He'll repeat that my mother made a thoughtless decision and I'll agree, nodding my head, waiting for the sermon to end so I can ask him what I've been wanting to ask for a while now: "Have you heard from my cousin?" But my grandfather won't answer; my grandfather doesn't answer. He just says, "I don't know," and he grabs his briefcase, gets up from the desk, and goes to his room. "Good-night," he says, and disappears behind a door.

It was one of those nights, one of those stories. I don't know how we got there, but my mom started talking about my Uncle Neno, recalling the days she'd spent with him. And I asked her to tell me about the accident again, and that's where it all started. She looked at me and told me that someday she'd tell me the truth, but that for now, I wouldn't be able to understand. That's what she told me: that I couldn't understand the truth. Then we sat in silence. The interview was over, and we went to bed. After that we never did the radio program again. Coka went back outside. It was during that time that she stopped eating and started to whimper.

The TV is on, tuned to a channel that has no signal. There's a faint buzzing sound. The chairs are in disarray. There are a couple of beer cans next to one of them. I walk slowly, trying not to make noise. I don't know which room the men are sleeping in; no lights are on. My shadow grows diffuse on the floor. I move toward my room. I hear a whimper. It's coming from the room next to mine. It's not the sound of sobbing, but at times it almost seems like it is. I decide to keep walking. I go into my room, turn on the lamp, and sit on the bed. My plan is to go to Morro the next day and look for Aldo, who knew my cousin. I lie down and close my eyes. And then it comes to me: the image of my mom lying down, facing away from me, her back red and sweaty.

When the interviews ended, we felt a bit strange. The first few days, we talked about it before we went to sleep. That's why the stories started. We needed to go on with the questions and answers, but our hearts weren't in it anymore. Now we just wanted to tell stories, to talk. And then my Uncle Neno came up again.

The sun is beating in through the window of my room. It wakes me up; the place is unbearable. I get up and go downstairs. Grandpa isn't there. I pour myself a glass of juice. It's around noon. I call my dad to find out where my grandpa is. He tells me it's Monday, and on Mondays he goes to the cemetery. I hang up. I think I'll just have to cook for myself. I had to learn the last time I came to Iquique, right after my grandmother died. My mom sent me a notebook with recipes. I cooked every day, and my grandfather always found some flaw. Too much salt, not enough salt, the absolute absence of salt. Things like that. But I didn't listen to him. I guess I'll have to cook again now. I don't know what to make. I open the refrigerator and there's nothing there. I leave the kitchen and sit down at the table. I drink a little juice. I turn on the TV, then turn it off again. I look for a phone book but can't find one. I don't remember Aldo's last name. My grandpa gets home and I ask him if he has a phone book. He says no and goes into the kitchen. He puts on an apron and starts to peel some potatoes.

The story I knew: My uncle had been driving all night. In the morning, he changed places with the alternate and went to lie down. They were on the last stretch of desert. The truck was carrying goods from Santiago: fruit, vegetables, groceries. And it was going fast. Maybe faster than it should have been. But there were no onlookers or witnesses. Just the open desert and the highway and the open sky, blue and open. The truck advanced toward Iquique. They had to go through Humberstone. Then the desert, more earth, until they saw the ocean, the city, Iquique. But first there was a car. No mention of color or any identifying details. Just that a friend of the family was driving it. A man who worked in a bank and who knew the truck that was going so fast belonged to my grandpa. And he was behind it, and tried to pass a few times, but he couldn't. He was watching it, searching for the right moment, but no. It was going very fast. He stopped trying and stayed behind the truck. He wasn't in a hurry. He watched it. It was a long truck. Suddenly, a silhouette on the driver's side of the truck, hanging on. The open door. The truck that kept going without slowing down. The silhouette pressed against the side of the truck, looking down at the highway. Then jumping. The man in the car braked. He sat still for a moment, as if someone had pressed pause. The frozen image. The desert. The explosion. Play. The man pressed the accelerator again. He made it to Iquique. My family. Everyone driving into the desert. The sound of ambulances. The fire.

I have lunch with my grandpa. "Don't drink so much soda," he tells me. I pick up the glass and walk to the sink. I turn on the tap and fill the glass with water, then go back to the table. He asks when I'm going to see my grandmother. I tell him I'll go soon, that I really don't know what one does at the cemetery. My grandpa observes me for a moment in silence, then turns his head from left to right and looks back down at his plate. I've never understood death, I think to myself. I'd like to tell him that, to tell him and my dad that I've never known what it means for someone to die. They must know. He must know. But I don't. I guess I'll only understand it when my mom dies. Although maybe not even that will be enough.

"When are you and your father going to Tacna?" my grandpa asks, and I shrug my shoulders.

"You should go soon," he says. "Just imagine if you lost all your teeth." I nod and go on eating.

"That's all a lie," said my mom.

He appears on the threshold. A tall man with short white hair, a moustache, blue eyes, a broad forehead. His head almost touches the ceiling. I think he must be well over six feet tall. He greets my grandpa, and they talk about something I can't make out. Then the man leaves. I hear the slam of a door closing. Grandpa tells me the man has been at the boarding house for a few months, that he's from Russia or some country over there, that he's never understood the man well, but he's a good guy. He says he's seen him reading the Bible in his room, and that makes him trustworthy. Because a man who reads the Bible, says my grandpa, is a man who would never do harm, because he follows the teachings of Jehovah, who art in heaven.

I remember how in Buenos Aires I saw my dad reading the Bible and *La Atalaya,* that Jehovah's Witness magazine. He read them when everyone else had gone to sleep, in that hotel room in downtown Buenos Aires. But I couldn't sleep; the heat was a constant pounding in my head, like being hungover, or that's what I was thinking when I opened my eyes and saw him reading those things by the bedside lamp. And he didn't notice me, he went on reading until he finally turned off the light, and I watched the dawn over Buenos Aires while his son snored nonstop.

The real story is different. Of course, my mother skipped over details when she told it to me. She uttered the word "accident" many times, like someone asking forgiveness. Then she told me to keep the secret, saying it wasn't worth it to keep going over the thing. She said it like that, in the tone of someone telling a story that doesn't matter to anyone.

I have to look for Aldo, to ask him if he knows where my cousin might be. I grab my wallet and walk toward the ocean. I have to get to Morro, walk for a while along the beach, and then pay a visit to the apartments where I grew up. I don't know if you'd call it a tenement, but it sure seemed like one. Five-story buildings. Apartment blocks, and they were right at the edge of the water, but you couldn't go swimming because there were so many rocks. My block was A2, which, along with A1, was the biggest in Morro. Although the good thing about the A2 block was that it had a direct view of the sea. It looked like one of those postcards they sell in the markets. It sounds cliché, but that's what the view was like when you came out of the apartment. The rocks, the sea, the sun. Of course, that didn't matter to us kids. We only worried about the hoods who came to dive off a kind of dock that had been built to keep back the constant pounding of the waves. That was also the place where some men went to fish, but we didn't care about that either. We were only concerned with making sure the hoods didn't get us; we were always hiding. We were like rats: sometimes we'd be playing soccer on the Morro field, and if we saw the hoods coming our way, we'd scurry off and disappear among the buildings. When we saw them heading back to Jorge Inostroza, everything returned to normal.

The night she told me the story, I had a hard time fall-ing asleep afterwards. I kept thinking about my cousin, who was just over a year old when it all happened. I won-dered what she would do if I told her the truth. How would she react? Maybe she'd murder my father. That's what I thought, absurd as it was. Or maybe she'd send him to jail. Those were the possibilities, out-of-control reactions. But my mom insisted that I keep quiet, that nothing was going to change now. "o.k.," I said, and I closed my eyes. That night I dreamed about my dad. He was a giant whale flying over Santiago. There were two Chilean ships chasing him. The city was deserted. The whale went all over Santiago and moaned the whole time. It was a blue whale, and it was headed toward the Andes Mountains. Harpoons started fly-ing from the ships toward the whale. One of them pierced its left side. The whale fell into the snow, as if it had run aground. There were more harpoons. Red snow. Black sky. The whale kept moaning. I opened my eyes, and the sound went on. My mom was in the yard. Coka was stretched out on the ground, shaking.

Part of the story I'd almost forgotten: the group of friends who lived in A2. There were five of us. I was the youngest. After I left Iquique, I never saw them again. I remember them well, though I don't know if they would recognize me now. Over ten years have passed. They must not remember anything. They must not remember what happened the last day, the day we stopped seeing each other for good.

Coka whined all night long. I managed to sleep for a couple of hours anyway. When I woke up, I decided not to go to class. My mom didn't say anything. I spent the whole day in bed. I started watching videos from the most recent Champions League finals. I didn't have the energy to do any commentary. My mom left the recorder and microphone beside the bed. I picked up the machine and started listening to some old recordings. I stopped on one of the interviews I'd done with my mother. In it, she talked about my brother, about the few minutes she'd gotten to spend with him. "Today," said my mother, "he'd be the same age as your cousin."

Supposedly he was Uruguayan, or that's what he said. His mother had been born in Montevideo and had fallen in love with a Chilean doctor. They got married there, had two children, and then came to Iquique. That's where Antonio was born. We met when I arrived at block A2. He was thin, tall, and blond. He was probably fifteen years old, like the others, and I was eight or nine. At first we barely spoke. I just listened to his mother laugh and talk loudly, in her marked Uruguayan accent, while they walked their five dogs. I'm not sure, but I think Aldo introduced us in his apartment. We were playing Super Nintendo, and Antonio came over with his mother. She sat talking with Aldo's mom, and Antonio came in and sat down with us. I think we were playing Mortal Kombat. In the afternoon we went down to the parking lot and tried to get a baseball game going. Aldo talked to boys from the other buildings and we managed to get some people together. That day we met Claudio and his brother and we formed our group. We didn't have a name, but the five of us were always on the same team. A while after that, we built a clubhouse out of palm branches, but the wind knocked it down. We rebuilt it, but it was no use. At night the tide came in, and the city changed completely. We were all waiting for the tsunami we'd heard so much about to hit, the moment we least expected it.

I listened to the interview twice. At first my mother answered the way she always did, leaving loose ends, silences, the kind of thing that seems so much a part of her life. I think we talked about that once, in a different interview. About abusing silences, not telling what she had to tell fully. She said she didn't know how to do it any other way, that she needed someone to ask her and then ask her again. That's why the story about my brother was different: no omissions, no skipping over things. She accepted the question and began: "He was going to have the same name as you. He was going to have both your names, and the room you grew up in was going to be his." Then she was quiet. In the recording, you can hear a whispering sound. Maybe a car parking outside the apartment. Then she said, "But he wasn't born." And again she was silent for a few seconds, until she said that it had all been my grandfather's fault. Or my grandparents'. The whispering, the sound of the phone, and the tape ran out.

The beach comes into view. Bellavista is unchanged. There are some sun umbrellas and a couple of boys trying to catch a wave with their surfboards. We used to try to do that sometimes too. The last summer we were together, that's how we spent all our time. I would wake up before ten, and I'd go pick them up one by one. Of course, we used bodyboards, not surfboards. We'd walk to Bellavista, and we'd settle in the calmest spot. I don't know anymore what it was called. I just remember the name of one section: Pepita de Oro. Supposedly no one surfed there because there were a lot of rocks and the waves got up to fifteen feet high. Supposedly if you went in, you didn't come out. Supposedly there was a gringo who once managed to ride a couple of waves, but then he disappeared. Of course, sometimes we'd walk along the rocks until we reached Pepita de Oro. We'd sit down still holding our boards, and we'd spend all afternoon watching the waves break. When the sun started to set, we'd go back to our building. Then we'd usually shower and then get together to play Super Nintendo, or watch some *Dragon Ball Z* movie. That's how our afternoons slipped past. My mom would come home at night, after work, and she'd ask me about the things I'd done during the day. Before she went to bed, she always asked me if I had called my dad. And always, I think, I shook my head no.

That afternoon, I kept listening to the tapes. My mom talking about my dad, about my grandparents, always bringing up her childhood. But I couldn't concentrate. I just sat there thinking about my cousin and my brother, their similar ages. I imagined them growing up together, their lives coinciding with each other. I started to think about what his life would have been like. About his tastes, whether he would have had problems shopping for clothes because he was overweight. Or how we would have gotten along. Or about the difference in our ages. According to her, she didn't think about him; she wasn't interested in imagining anything. That's what she said on one of the tapes, and the conversation ended there, abruptly, with her saying it wasn't worth it, there was no point.

Although the truth is, we spent almost all our time playing baseball. That last year in Morro, I watched the whole World Series. It was on late, close to midnight. The New York Yankees were the champions. I never learned the players' names or what their positions were called. The only important thing, the only thing that mattered to us, was hitting the tennis ball as hard as possible and running, running fast around all the bases. Sometimes we tried to steal one, but that never worked for me. By the time I got to first base I was already a wreck, and I'd just stay there, panting, my hands on my knees, waiting for Claudio or Antonio to hit the ball hard, so hard it would land on the roof of one of the buildings: home run. The game would end—we didn't have any more tennis balls, it was growing dark, the waves were starting to crash in hard—and we would all go back into our apartments.

When night fell, my mom came into my room and told me Coka was still crying. We went to the yard and there she was, thin, her cocker spaniel ears covered in dirt. She was lying in her house and crying. "I don't know what to do," said my mom.

"Me neither." I knelt down and started to pet her side. She closed her eyes and was quiet. "Let's go to bed," said my mom. "It's really cold." We went into the apartment. I lay down beside her. She embraced me and asked me if I was o.k. "All o.k.," I said, and I gave her a kiss on the forehead. She hugged me harder, moving so our bodies were close together. Her head smelled like hair dye. She started to sob. The TV was on, the evening dramas.

"What's wrong?" I asked her.

I pass the El Castillo bakery. I see a public phone and stop. I know I should call my mother, ask her how she's doing. But I don't want to. I put two coins in and dial. It's busy. Luckily. I know she'll ask me about the list of things I haven't bought. She'll tell me to insist. They've put in some new signs along the streets. They're green and they have a wave drawn on them. Underneath, the word "tsunami." I call my mother again, but no one answers. I give it one last try, but she still doesn't answer. The sun is beating down. There's the sound of the waves crashing in the distance. I stop and stand there for a moment. I look at the new signs. When I was little, we were all waiting for the tidal wave to hit. Or a tsunami. In school we practiced Operation Deyse: Imagine the earth was starting to tremble, everyone under the benches, protecting our heads with our hands. Then evacuate the building and, without losing our calm, go running toward the hills. Over and over we practiced. The tidal wave never came, the tsunami never came. But for a long time, we went on practicing Operation Deyse.

That night she talked about my father and how lonely she felt. She turned out the light, and we were left in the dark. She told me I had no idea what it was like to be left alone. "Because you're going to leave," she said. "You're going to pack up your things, and you'll leave."

"I don't know," I replied as she pulled the sheets over her face. It was a slow and awkward gesture. She told me no one was ever going to want a woman like her, and she asked me to hold her tight again. I obeyed, and she was quiet. I felt her bulky belly against my own. She asked me to run my fingers through her hair, and once again, I obeyed.

The tennis court no longer exists. The grounds are empty. There are just some traces of clay left. The multipurpose court is still there, though. Some boys are playing a game while a girl tries to shoot into one of the hoops. Sometimes she talks to the goalie. They must be ten years old, maybe twelve. They talk, and the ball stays far away from the goal. I start to walk down toward the A2 block. I leave the field behind, and the ocean comes into view. There are still palm trees leading to the building's parking lot. I get closer, and now I see the apartment where I lived. There's a sign that says FOR RENT. It's on the ground floor. I can hear the waves breaking against the pier. I don't know if there are people fishing. I don't know if there are any hoods diving into the water. I just stand there looking at the building. I look at the apartments where the others lived, and my eyes stop at Antonio's. Fifth floor. I still remember his father jumping. The impact. The sound of his bones when he hit the ground. Then my closed eyes. Then the screams and the sound of the ambulance. The Uruguayan woman's sobbing. Antonio slept somewhere else; he didn't come home that night. Not the next either. They left him with some of his cousins. Only when they were holding vigil over the body did they finally tell him. And Antonio did nothing, said nothing.

It was a light touch. Then a movement and another touch. She took my hand and brought it between her soft, fat thighs. I couldn't bend my fingers. "Keep petting my hair," she said as I started to feel the dampness, my fingers slightly sticky. She started to rock, and I still couldn't bend my fingers.

The night of the burial, Antonio slept at my house. The Uruguayan woman came over and started talking to my mom. We played Super Nintendo. An NBA game. I was the Minnesota Timberwolves. Antonio was the Los Angeles Lakers. And while we were playing, the Uruguayan woman was guzzling a bottle of pisco she'd gone out to buy. My mom just looked at her while she drank and talked about how she'd be going back to Montevideo, how now she had no reason to stay in this fucking country. I remember I heard that part clearly because she shouted it, and Antonio and I looked at each other for a few seconds while Kevin Garnett tried to make a basket. Then the Uruguayan woman laughed out loud, and we went on playing until we got sleepy, and we turned off the console, switched out the light, crawled under the covers, and slept. The next day my mom would tell me they'd had to take the Uruguayan woman to the hospital. She'd drunk a whole bottle of pisco, her blood pressure had plummeted, and an ambulance had come to the apartment. The medics knew her; they had worked with her husband. They berated my mom. They asked her, didn't she know the woman wasn't supposed to drink? My mom shook her head. Then they took the Uruguayan away. My mom turned out the lights in the apartment and went to sleep.

Light was shining in through the window, and I could see her back. I got up and opened the window. A cold breeze came in. I got goosebumps. Coka started to cry louder, as if someone were hitting her. I shushed her, but it didn't work. I closed the window. I lay down beside my mother again. She was snoring, her bare back turned to me, red and sweaty.

There are two men fishing. A boy runs from side to side and throws stones into the ocean. The apartment is empty. No curtains on the windows. I have to call my mother. I have to buy the clothes on the list. The boy goes on throwing stones, and one of the men begins doing the same. I go into the building. Up to the top floor. I sit down on the stairs, right across from the apartment where Antonio used to live. The smell of dog shit is gone now. I hear a door open on the floor below; it's the apartment where Aldo lived. I wonder if I should move, if I should see if it's him, but instead I stay seated on the stairs, as if I were waiting for someone. That last day, when it all happened, the door was half open. Antonio's brother had taken the dogs for a walk. I couldn't hear anyone. I went in because I needed to ask Antonio to lend me some games. I went in slowly and there they were, on the bed. She was crying and emitting a low whine. Antonio was on top of her, rocking. I thought he was trying to kill her. It seemed like he was crying too. Then she let out a shrill cry and they embraced. I turned around that instant and ran out of the apartment. I never saw my friends again.

I kept my eyes closed for a long time. I didn't want to wake up, but a siren had started to wail outside the apartment. On the night table, there was a tray with a mug and a sandwich. Under the mug was a note: "I went shopping for lunch. Don't sleep too late. Take care of Coka. xo." Outside, the day was cloudy. It was close to noon. I rubbed both hands over my face, then got up and opened the window. Coka was lying on the ground, panting. I called her name, but she didn't even move. I went to my room to get clothes. Then I showered, got dressed, left a note saying I'd be back late, and went out. On the bus I started thinking about where I could go for lunch. Some restaurant downtown. Anywhere, really. The most important thing right then was to eat something big, something that would hold me over until very late. I got off at the University of Chile stop and started walking down Paseo Ahumada. A McDonald's. El Nuria. I reached Plaza de Armas and went into the Fernández Concha building. I thought about having a couple of hot dogs, but I didn't want to eat standing up. What I wanted was to sit down for a while, eat calmly, let the afternoon progress. I kept walking, now down Paseo Estado: another McDonald's, a Kentucky Fried Chicken, a Telepizza, a Burger King. I walked as far as Alameda, turned around, and finally went into the KFC.

I hear some footsteps going down the stairs. Someone's come out of the apartment where Aldo used to live. I go over to the railing and try to see if it's him, but I only hear the footsteps. I go downstairs and stop in front of his door. I know he can't still be living here. I know it won't be him or his mother or his aunt who opens the door for me. A stranger will open the door and tell me that all the people living in the building are new. Antonio and the Uruguayan aren't there, nor are Claudio and his brother. I turn around and start to go down the stairs. I think Aldo probably wouldn't remember my cousin anyway. Or maybe he would, but most likely he'd have lost track of her. It's logical. They were classmates at school, but that doesn't mean anything. I keep going down the stairs, and I leave the building. The men and the boy are still on the dock. It's getting dark. There's a ship off in the distance. I have to meet up with my father tonight. We have to plan the trip to Tacna. I walk toward the dock to see what they're catching. I get closer and the men say something to each other. The boy keeps throwing stones into the ocean. I look down and see two sea lions with their heads sticking out of the water. The boy is throwing stones at them, and they duck underwater. I watch for a few seconds as the sun goes down. I leave the dock and head back to my grandpa's house.

I ordered a crispy chicken sandwich with avocado, some nuggets, french fries, cheese empanadas, and a large soda. I tore off four restaurant vouchers and handed them to the cashier. They gave me my order and I went to sit on the second floor. There weren't many people. A couple, a father with his son, a few students. I sat down as far away from the other people as I could and started in on the french fries. First I opened a packet of ketchup and another of mustard and dumped them onto the paper tray liner. I picked up a knife and mixed them together. First went the french fries, then the empanadas. In between I took bites of the chicken sandwich and dipped the nuggets in the ketchup and mustard mixture. I ate fast, as if someone were rushing me. I took a sip of soda and went on. At one point a girl in a KFC uniform appeared. She started to collect some of the trays the customers had left on the tables. She was very white, with brown hair and a tiny nose. She was tiny, thin. She picked up the trays and dumped them into the garbage. More people started to arrive. She cleared the tables and went back to the ground floor. Then another woman came; she was older, maybe fifty. She was short and moved slowly. She offered to take my tray and the scraps of food. I told her not to worry about it. Then she took the garbage bags, which were full, and changed them out for new ones. I sat there drinking my soda, which by then was mixed with the water from the ice. Faded soda. I stayed sitting there for a while. I thought about going to buy another combo meal, or maybe changing restaurants. I still had vouchers left, so money wasn't a problem. The soda was gone; I chewed the ice. More people came, and they started to look at me. I got up and left the restaurant.

I go back to the boarding house on the same road I took to Morro, thinking about how I have to see about the trip to Tacna. I look at the field. I hear shouting. The boys who'd been playing football are arguing with some bigger boys who aren't wearing shirts. The boys look at each other and start to run toward where I am. The hoods start to chase them. They're coming toward me. I start running too. The boys don't talk, they just run, and I try to follow them. Behind us the hoods are coming, yelling that they're going to kill us. The boys leave me behind. I start gasping for breath. I remember the days when I had to jog in high school, when I had to run laps around the block. Five times around in under ten minutes. They were huge blocks; it took me over twenty. I'd end up red, panting like I am now, as I avoid looking behind me. I still haven't lost sight of the boys; they go into one of the buildings. I follow them. I see the hoods go past me. They go up the stairs. "Stay there, fucking rat," one of them says to me. He pushes me. I fall. "Where are those fucking kids?" he asks me. I say something he doesn't understand and he starts kicking me, I hear a door slam, he keeps kicking me in the ribs. I cover my mouth, the only thing I'm worried about is protecting my mouth, I don't care about anything else, I imagine my teeth scattering; he goes on kicking me in the ribs, in the thighs, I close my eyes, I feel more kicks, my teeth, my mouth, the taste of dirt, shouting.

I walked downtown for a while, waiting for dusk to fall. Before returning to the apartment, I went back to the Fernández Concha building and ate a combo meal, two hot dogs and a soda. I spent two vouchers. The people around me were all office workers. All of them eating quickly, drinking beer, laughing. I left, caught the bus, and arrived at the apartment when it was already getting dark. The lights were off. My mom was sleeping with a blanket over her; the smell that had been there in the morning was still there. I went out to the yard to see Coka. She was still lying on the ground, trembling. Now she didn't even let out a whine; she just shook with her eyes closed. I knelt down and petted her head. "I haven't been able to get her inside," said my mother, suddenly. "She tried to bite me." She was there, in the doorway to the yard in her pajamas, looking at me.

"We should put her down," I said, and she took it badly. She yelled at me, asked if I was sick, told me she hadn't raised a son of a bitch. I was quiet. I'd never thought the dog meant so much to her. She never liked Coka before; in fact, when I brought her to the apartment, she told me the dog could only stay for a few days. I picked her up from the ground; she let out a low growl, and I brought her inside. She opened her eyes: a thin white film covered them. My mom stopped yelling and went back to her room. She turned on the TV. I went to my room, closed the door, and lay down.

I touch my teeth to see if they're loose. They're o.k. One of my ribs hurts, and my legs. I get up and brush myself off. The boys shout down to me and ask if I'm o.k. I look up and tell them I am, not to worry. One of them comes down and says I can come into his apartment, clean myself up in his bathroom. I'm limping. I climb the stairs slowly and go inside. They tell me I got off easy, that these hoods are always trying to beat them up, that they'd had a problem once and they've been after them ever since. I go to the bathroom and stand in front of the mirror. I open my mouth, check my teeth. They look yellower than usual. I touch them again to see if any of them came loose. No, they're firmly in place. I splash water on my face and lift up my shirt. My left ribs hurt a lot. I wet a towel and pass it over the spot. Then I come out of the bathroom and thank the boys. I walk, limping, from Morro to my grandpa's boarding house: the hoods stole my wallet.

The next day we had breakfast together. That was when she brought up the idea of calling my grandpa and asking him if I could spend some time in Iquique. I said o.k. In the end I had to call myself. My dad answered. He told me about his trip to Buenos Aires and asked me if I wanted to go with him. I said yes.

"That's how the world is," says my grandpa. "Great Babylon is king, but Jehovah, who art in heaven, will take care of those who follow his word. That's why we have to read the Bible," he tells me while I drink a cup of tea. "We have to educate ourselves so we can vanquish Satan."

I nod my head and make a sandwich. I think eating will help me get better. I cut the bread in half and take out a slice of ham. My grandpa asks why I don't eat some crackers instead. I tell him I'm hungry, and I take a little butter. I spread it on the bread, and he tells me I'm going to have a heart attack if I keep eating like that. I leave the knife to one side and put a slice of ham on the bread. Now he's talking to me about Jehovah's Witnesses. He asks me if we open the door when they come to our apartment in Santiago. I tell him that we do, that I've even invited them into the living room and offered them tea. My grandpa smiles and says, "That's very good." I nod again and smile. The doorbell rings. "Must be Mirna," he says, and he gets up to open the door.

My mother knew I didn't want to go back to Iquique. We were in agreement on that. Although she was more adamant: "I wouldn't go back to that city even if I were dead," she told me in one of the interviews, when we were talking about her dad. He'd lived in Iquique too, he'd also had to get out suddenly, and he'd also decided never to go back. It was a strange thing, but true.

After that night, we didn't sleep together anymore. I almost never went to class. I locked myself in my room to listen to old recordings, from when we'd talked about my Uncle Neno, when we'd talked about Iquique, about our last days at my grandpa's house, about the possibility that everything could have been different. "But it was impossible," my mom would say, and then she'd change the subject. All the same, I kept thinking about it.

My grandpa leaves me alone with Ms. Mirna while he gets ready to go to the Kingdom Hall. She's a Jehovah's Witness, too, but she belongs to a different congregation. She drinks a cup of tea while I watch TV. Since my grandmother died, Ms. Mirna takes care of the boarding house. I'll find all this out a little later, when my grandpa calls me into his room and tells me who she is. He'll also tell me about her granddaughter, who disappeared in Alto Hospicio. Then he'll put on his jacket and leave for the Kingdom Hall, and I'll be left with Ms. Mirna while I wait for my dad to call. The phone won't ring until ten at night. Before that, Ms. Mirna will tell me the story of her granddaughter, like someone putting together and taking apart a worn-out puzzle.

First Nancy came along. The separation. Then my father's son. Still, everything was fine. My mom had a candy distribution business; she sold wholesale. She did well. But then came the Asian financial crisis, and everything was fucked. Businesses started to close, people didn't go out anymore. And things started going badly for my mom, while for my dad, they started to go well. Back then he was living in Santiago with his new family, and he'd bought a truck he used for transporting fruits and vegetables. One day my mom called him and told him she didn't have the money to pay for my school. My dad said he didn't either. They sat for a few seconds in silence, phones to their ears, and then they hung up. At the same time. After that I went to live with my grandpa, and my mom came too, a month later. We lived there, shut up in a room on the second floor. Sometimes my grandmother would come up to see how we were. My grandpa didn't say much. He was just happy we were there with him. But nothing improved. Until winter vacation came and my mom shipped me off to Santiago to stay with some nephew of hers I'd never met. A few days later, I opened the door of that house and saw her there. She was wearing sunglasses and had a bandage around her left wrist. She was carrying a bag and seventy thousand pesos. "I left everything else in Iquique," she told my cousin. My grandparents didn't understand what had happened. Two years had passed by the time they found out we were living in Santiago. And she made that promise: to never go back to Iquique.

First of all, she never speaks as if her granddaughter is dead. No. Her granddaughter disappeared. Her granddaughter, according to her, is going to come back one day. She's sure about that; that's why she doesn't believe the story about the Alto Hospicio psychopath. "That man is innocent," she tells me. "That man is atoning for something else, something from before, but he's got nothing to do with it. My girl disappeared, but she's going to come back, I'm sure of it, because at night, when I can't sleep, I hear her voice. I hear her talk to me and ask for my help, I hear her say, 'Granny, I'm scared,' and I talk to her, I cry out to her, I tell her not to worry, that I'll help her. Then she doesn't say anything and I can hear her crying," Ms. Mirna tells me. "And I can't sleep, there are whole weeks when I can't sleep. I walk around the house and I start thinking about her, and I pray to Jehovah, who art in heaven, and ask him to bring her back to me. But sometimes her crying doesn't stop, and sometimes I pray— but don't you tell anyone this, my boy—sometimes I pray to the Virgin Mary, because she knows what it's like to lose a child. Because she was my *child,* not my grandchild, she was my daughter, and she disappeared. But I know she's going to come back. I'm sure they'll let her go someday," says Ms. Mirna, and her voice wanes as we listen to the ticking of a big clock hanging on the wall.

My mother and I just left, from one day to the next. Bounced checks left behind. The storeroom full of empty boxes. My dad was the one who realized we were gone. He'd known things were going badly. He'd started a new job selling plastic products, and the repository was near my mother's shop. He knew, but he did nothing. He only reacted when he saw her closed-up shop. Supposedly my grandpa went to prison for a few days because of the checks. Supposedly the creditors went to my grandpa's house to get the money from him and threatened to kill him. But none of that can be proven. It's just the story my dad and my grandpa told me, the story they made up, from which they omitted one important part. Because later we found out they'd told everyone we'd taken off with a lot of money, that my mom's goal had been to screw them over. They thought—and they spread the word—that we'd left with ten million pesos, that we were in the South, that we were happy, that we deserved to go to hell; that's what my grandpa said. That was the story. That was their story.

"They took her because she was pretty," says Mirna. "They took her because she was smart and didn't talk much; they took her to Peru, to Bolivia. They took her to Sucre, La Paz, Tacna, or Lima," says Ms. Mirna, eyes closed and hands together. "They took her, and they don't want to give her back to me." She starts to sob. Of course, I don't know what to say to her. She doesn't speak again. She keeps her hands pressed together and starts to murmur something I don't understand. I hear footsteps. It's the Russian. She opens her eyes and sits, looking at him. The Russian starts to say something, but then she starts sobbing. It's a loud, hoarse howl. There are no tears, only the howl, and the Russian looks at us and then turns around and leaves. He looks like a giant robot, I think. I get up and pour a glass of water. I give it to Ms. Mirna, but she doesn't stop howling.

The phone rings. It's my dad.

When my grandmother died, my grandpa called my mom to tell her to return to Iquique.

"I need you two," he said. "I don't want to be alone." My mom didn't say anything at first. She thought of asking him about his son, why he didn't tell his son to go and keep him company. But she chose not to argue. My grandpa insisted we come back, but she held firm. She told him about her promise, how she wouldn't go back even dead.

Ms. Mirna apologizes to me. She says sometimes these things come over her and she can't control herself. "It's all right," I tell her. I put on a sweatshirt and say good-bye to her. "May Jehovah keep you," she tells me. I take a bus that drops me off at my father's address. It's a condominium. Four towers, each with many floors. The concierge calls my dad's apartment and lets me go up. It's nighttime. In the middle of the towers are three very large pools, their lights turned on. Three girls are swimming, and I see Elías with them. "Bro, over here," he shouts, and I keep walking. Nancy opens the door for me. She sees I'm limping as I enter and she asks me if I'm o.k. "No," I tell her. I walk past her. My dad is lying down and watching a soccer rerun. I sit on his bed. He asks me why I went nosing around Morro. I tell him about my cousin, that I want to talk to her. He doesn't say anything. He comments on the game. "Looks like we're going to go to Tacna sooner than I thought," he tells me. "I came into a little money, so we can go and you can get that mouth of yours looked at."

"Yeah, I'm bleeding more and more," I tell him, and he tells me that's what I get for not taking care of myself, that it's dangerous, I could lose my teeth.

"And do you know how I can find my cousin?"

"No," he says. "What do you want with her?"

"I don't know. I want to talk to her."

"Your cousin doesn't live here anymore," he says. "She left a long time ago with her family." It sounds big, numerous, the word "family." I'd like to ask him what he means, but I don't get the chance. He makes another comment on the game he's watching.

Before the trip to Buenos Aires, I listened to the last recordings again. The days my mom spent with my Uncle Neno.
The times she'd had to go pick him up, at dawn, at some
bars where he'd fallen asleep. Or when they'd go to the
movies. The kind of thing my dad didn't like to do. Or
the day he finally got married. "He didn't want to," my mom
said. "The only thing he wanted was to get out of there."
At one point he proposed it. He asked my mom to help
him get away, said they could take her car, travel south. She
could stay with him at first, and then she could go back;
he couldn't do it alone. But my mom didn't dare. My Uncle
Neno got married, and there was no honeymoon or anything. Months later my cousin was born. A year after that,
my uncle died.

I lie down next to my dad and fall asleep. After a while the woman wakes me up, saying it's late, she wants to go to bed. My dad is snoring. I don't know how I'll get back. "Call a cab," she says. I don't want to move. "I don't know the number for any," I reply. "I'll call you one," she says, and she leaves the room. I get up and follow her. Elías asks me if I want to play his Nintendo Wii with him. I look at the console for a moment. I tell him no. The taxi arrives. I go back to my grandpa's house. I find him in the living room, reading the Bible. He asks me if everything was O.K. with Ms. Mirna. I tell him yes. "I feel sorry for the sister," says my grandpa. "All day long, talking about her granddaughter. But Jehovah, who art in heaven, must be keeping her safe in the Kingdom of Heaven. Because she was a good girl; she was quiet," says my grandpa. "But Satan is powerful, almost as powerful as Jehovah, and that's why we have to be watchful, son, because one never knows when temptation will fall upon us. We must be strong and read the Bible," he says, and he gets up from his desk, picks up his cane, and heads for his room. He turns out the light in the living room and tells me good-night. The thud of the door. I sit down on a chair and wait there for a while. Every so often I hear the sound of a car speeding by. Outside the house there's a sign that says O'HIGGINS BOARDING HOUSE. The living room is awash in blue from the sign and from the streetlights. One of my ribs hurts. I lean my head back in the chair and close my eyes.

We went to Buenos Aires on a Monday morning. My dad came to pick me up at dawn with the woman and her son. He came into my house talking in an Argentinian accent, saying the taxi was waiting outside. The night before, my mom had given me the list of things I had to buy, kissed me on the forehead, and locked herself in her room. I hadn't slept at all when my dad arrived. Coka had been whining all night. I'd taken a chair, a blanket, my tape recorder, and the microphone and sat down next to her. When I put the microphone in front of her snout, she stopped crying. I spent the better part of the night petting her, recording her whining until she fell asleep. That morning, while my dad was waiting for me in the living room, I went to say good-bye to Coka. She had just come out of her house. She seemed to be in better spirits. She staggered toward her food bowl. White eyes, all bones, ears covered in dirt, paws trembling. I patted her head, picked up my bag, and went to the taxi.

The sun is coming up. I run a finger over my teeth. I'm bleeding. I go up to the room where my things are, change clothes, and go into the bathroom. I brush my teeth with extreme caution. I try to brush slowly and without much force, but I still bleed. I end up spitting out toothpaste mixed with blood. It doesn't hurt, but the taste stays stuck to the roof of my mouth. I try again. Brush slowly, more softly on the upper teeth. But again, I fail. I look at myself in the mirror. My mouth full of bloody toothpaste.

I sat next to my dad on the plane. His son and his wife sat in a different row. My dad watched a movie during the flight, and I listened to music. For a moment I thought I should ask him about my Uncle Neno. The whole time we were in Buenos Aires that idea nagged at me, but we never had a moment alone. That's what I wanted: for us to go out one day and talk. I hinted at it, but he didn't say anything. He just pretended not to notice.

It's a murmuring. Words I can't make out. I move closer to the room they're coming from, but I still can't make out what's happening. A foreign language. Through the window, I can see a small lamp. The light is very faint. A man is kneeling beside his bed. A murmur. I stay there a moment, listening as if I'm hypnotized.

I also thought about telling him what happened with my mom. I don't know why, but I had a feeling he would listen.

I open my eyes. I'm in the middle of the hallway. I taste the blood between my teeth. I get up quickly. The door to the room is open. There is no murmuring now. I move closer. The bed is made. There's nothing. There's no one.

I called my mom from the Buenos Aires Zoo. We had to go there because my dad's son got it into his head that we had to visit the zoo. I talked to my mom for a while, and she told me Coka was feeling better, that at least now she was eating a little. Then she asked me if I'd bought anything on my list. I told her I hadn't, that my dad had said he didn't have the money and we would buy everything in Iquique. Just then, the call got cut off.

I rinse my mouth and go down to my grandpa's room. It's around noon. He's not there. I walk toward the kitchen, and I find him there, wearing a white apron, stirring a pot with a wooden spoon. "That's why you're so fat," he tells me, "because you don't do any physical activity. Look at the time, and you're just getting up."

"I was reading," I tell him, and he bursts out laughing.

"You should go jogging on the beach, or for a walk. Otherwise you're going to die. Jehovah doesn't want men like you," he says. "He wants active men, ones who take care of their bodies, their souls, who know how to appreciate life. Good men," he says, and I stay quiet. The words I could say to him in reply won't stop spinning around in my head. There are a lot, they hound each other, they won't fall into place. "I'm going to have lunch at my dad's," I tell him, and I go back up to my room.

We went back to Santiago very early. On the plane I went over the list again and again. Jacket, pants, tennis shoes, shirts, underwear, socks. I looked at the list and then at Nancy. She and her son were watching a movie on the screen facing their seats. My dad was sleeping. At one point there was a lot of turbulence. I imagined the plane going down. My dad woke up and put his hand on my head. He slapped my back a couple of times while he laughed. "You're proud of your old dad, right?" he asked. The seat belt sign came on. The pilot announced we were arriving in Santiago de Chile. He gave the same instructions as always. The question was left hanging in the air. He forgot it and started talking to Nancy. I looked at the list and jotted down a few words that I then decided to erase.

Before I go to my dad's, I lie down for a moment on the bed. I lay my head back on my crossed arms. I look at the ceiling and think about my mother; maybe she's cooking too. Or playing solitaire on the computer, lighting a cigarette, then another and another. I close my eyes. The day before I left Iquique for Santiago, there was a party at my school. I remember it. That night, I know, I said I would never come back to Iquique. I said it to get attention, probably. But it doesn't matter. What matters is that party at the school. There she was, the girl I liked. I'd tried to choose my best clothes. Blue pants, a plaid shirt. I wanted to go up to her and tell her I liked her. I got to the school and started dancing with the girls in my class. Although really, I was a fifth wheel. They all had partners, and I just fumbled around and smiled. Moved my body. Sweated. I felt like my pants were really tight. And then she showed up holding hands with a guy who was older than us. They danced all night. She kissed him. My pants were still squeezing me. The fog started rolling in, and my classmates started leaving. She left with the older guy. The next day I'd get on the plane and leave for Santiago, for good. But something happened that day. It was an image that would repeat itself for years. Me dancing, no partner, in the middle of a group. Or pretending I was talking to someone on the phone while she went on dancing.

At the Santiago airport I ran into a girl from my class at the university. We were waiting in line to put our bags through the x-ray machines. My dad and his family were still waiting for their suitcases. We started talking, and she told me she'd been to Brazil with her parents. She asked me where I was coming from. I told her I'd gone to Argentina. "Nice," she said. "Did you go alone?" I was going to tell her no. Someone touched my back. It was my dad, with Nancy and her son. "Bro, who's she?" he asked. My classmate greeted each of them with a kiss on the cheek. I didn't say anything. It was her turn to drop her bag for them to inspect. She turned around and went forward. My dad's son repeated his question, and I still didn't answer him. My turn came, and I put my bag on the belt and went toward the door. My classmate was with her parents. She came over to say good-bye. She told me I looked a lot like my mom and my brother. I nodded. She kissed my cheek and left.

I have lunch with my dad and his family. We sit around the table: him, Nancy, Elías, Nancy's other two sons, and me. During lunch my dad talks about soccer and cars. That afternoon I fall asleep next to him in his bed. When I wake up, I tell him I don't want to go back to my grandpa's. He says o.k. That night I lie down on the sofa in the living room and sleep. I don't go back to my grandpa's the next day either.

My dad told me to call my mom and tell her we were back in Santiago. He handed me his phone and I dialed the number, but it was busy. I handed it back to him. We went out to get a taxi. When we were almost to the hotel where my dad was staying, Nancy asked for his cell phone. She called one of her kids. They talked for a moment. I never knew which one it was. I thought it might have been the oldest, the son who used to phone my mom to call her a whore, to tell her to leave my dad alone.

After several days I go back to my grandpa's house. My dad drops me off. They greet each other with a hug. My grandpa looks at me and asks me why I didn't come home sooner. I tell him that there's cable at my dad's, there's internet, that I get bored at his house. He shakes his head. He asks my dad if he's gone to see my grandmother. My dad tells him he hasn't had time. "None of you ever have time for anything," says my grandpa. My dad laughs and says good-bye. I stay standing there while my grandpa goes to lie down in his room. That night I hear the murmuring again, but this time it's coming from a different room. The same voice, the same words I don't understand, the man kneeling beside his bed.

We leave Santiago behind. The list. The trip through the desert. The man wandering in the hills, maybe lost. The man who listens to murmuring voices and drinks tea. Alto Hospicio. Iquique. The Russian. The missing girls. My cousin. My uncle. My mom. Bloody teeth. The trip to Tacna. The murmurs. My grandpa. Tight pants. The fog. Morro. The Uruguayan woman. My mom. The murmurs. I close my eyes, but I still hear them.

My grandpa keeps talking about the end of the world. My dad sometimes comes to see me. The trip to Tacna is approaching. My grandfather wakes me up very early so I can help him straighten up around the boarding house. Then I have to cook for him. Sometimes I go to my dad's apartment. When I get there, I find the woman's other sons are there too. Elías spends all day playing computer games. I arrive and lie down in my dad's room. I watch TV. I let the days pass. Sometimes I wish I could talk to him, but the woman is always there. I resign myself. I keep watching TV. It doesn't matter which channel. The trip to Tacna is approaching. It's been days since I called my mom.

I go to my dad's apartment again. Only Nancy's oldest son is there. I go inside, lock myself in the bedroom, and sleep. When my dad arrives, he asks me if I've eaten anything. I shake my head. He says he's hungry, that he didn't eat anything at Nancy's mom's house. He asks me if I feel like getting something to eat. I tell him yes. I put on a sweatshirt and we drive off in his truck. We go to a place that sells sandwiches. He slaps my back as we walk toward the place. We order two sandwiches and a large soda. We sit down. On TV they're showing a movie starring Denzel Washington. My dad talks about him, tells me he likes the one where Denzel plays a boxer, he likes that movie. We eat. He doesn't say anything after that. He watches the movie. We watch the movie. We finish eating. We go back to the truck, and my dad drops me off at my grandpa's. He pulls up in front of the boarding house and explains that he's in a hurry and tomorrow he'll come by to say hi. I get out and watch as the truck turns and disappears at the next corner. I go into the house and find my grandpa reading a magazine. I sit across from him, and he asks me how I've liked my time in Iquique. I reply that everything has been fine, and then I ask him if it's true that my dad killed my Uncle Neno.

My grandpa looks at me and tells me to stop talking nonsense, that I'm just a kid, that I don't understand anything, that I need to grow up. The next day he decides not to talk to me.

"We have to leave Iquique around six in the morning to make the most of the day in Tacna," my dad tells me. The woman and her son are coming with us. I pack my bag the night before. It's been days since I heard the murmuring. Ms. Mirna hasn't come back. Before going to bed, I look at the list of things my mom told me I had to buy. I'm going back to Santiago in two days, and I still haven't bought anything. Maybe I can find something in Tacna, I think, and I stash the list in my bag. The next day my dad shows up in the truck. He's alone. His son woke up with a fever. Nancy stayed to take care of him.

There's a Bob Dylan song on the radio. As we cross the desert, we lose the signal little by little. My dad looks at me out of the corner of his eye and he asks me if I'm o.k. I say yes and look out at the hills. They look like dragon cadavers buried in the desert. A dragon cemetery. That's what it looks like. But I don't say anything to my dad. The sun rises to its highest point in the sky. The highway is completely empty.

As we cross the hills that take us to Arica, I ask him about my Uncle Neno. I ask if he misses him, and he says yes. "But your mom must miss him more," he says, and I fall silent, not knowing very well what to add. The radio is playing an album by a jazz musician I don't know. We're close to Arica.

We cross the border into Tacna without any difficulty. They barely even look at the truck. As soon as we get there, I call my mom. I ask her how she is. She says not good; she doesn't have any money. She asks me if I've bought the clothes yet. I tell her no, that I'm in Tacna. She tells me to take advantage of being there and to buy shirts and other things. I ask about Coka. She says she's not doing well, that she's going to die. I'm silent. She repeats herself about the clothes, saying I should buy brand-name things. I tell her I have to go. I hang up. I leave the phone center and tell my dad everything is o.k. He slaps me on the back and tells me that I'll never forget these trips, that I've really been on some international vacations. I try to smile as I nod my head. I have a dentist appointment in a little while.

The dentist tells me I'm in bad shape, that if I'd waited a little longer I could have lost all my teeth. Like my mom, I think, while the dentist puts some pliers into my mouth and removes something unknown from my teeth. It takes a while. Then she smears a kind of paste on them. I look at her diplomas from the Catholic University of Peru. She hands me a mirror. My teeth are all red with blood, and the paste makes them look rotten. She calls my dad in. He looks at me and gives me two pats on the head. He says I'm going to be fine. She gives him a list of things he has to buy. I think of the list my mom sent with me.

We go back to the hotel early. I can't eat anything. My dad orders a sandwich that they bring up to the room. We lie down. There's another Denzel Washington movie on TV, and this time it's the one about the boxer. I close my eyes and imagine my dad buying me all the things on the list, that I go home and my mom doesn't scold me for not having bought this or that thing. That she doesn't inspect the clothes as if I'd bought them at a flea market. I open my eyes. The boxing movie is still on TV. My dad is snoring. I get up. I'm hungry. I don't know what to do. I turn off the TV and take the remote control out of my dad's hands. I also take off his glasses, put them on the night table, and turn off the light.

You can't see my teeth, just dough covered in blood. Supposedly it will fall off over the next few days. I can't eat until that happens, until there's no dough left. I look at my teeth in the bathroom mirror. My dad gets up and tells me not to worry, the dentist is very good.

It's early. He gets dressed and orders breakfast to the room.

After a while we go out and visit a couple of shopping centers. I have the list in my pocket. Nancy told my dad to buy some underwear for her kids and some tennis shoes for Elías. We went all over Caprina looking for them. I take the chance to try to find a pair for myself. I also look for other things from the list. My dad asks me if I need underwear and socks. I say yes. We go on looking for the tennis shoes for his son. Meanwhile, I try on a few pairs, but I don't like any of them. Finally my dad decides on a pair. I know I have to buy the shoes in that store; there won't be another chance. I try on another pair, and they're a little tight, but I don't care. I ask him if I can get them. "But didn't your grandpa buy you shoes?" I shake my head no. In the end, he buys them.

It's getting dark. I go with my dad to another shopping center. He buys things for his business. I look at the list. I ask my dad for a pen. I check off the words "tennis shoes." We go to another store. Now we're looking for the underwear Nancy asked him for. We arrive at a shop, and my dad greets a woman. He tells me to pick out the underwear and socks that I want. I throw them into a bag with the ones he picked out, and we go back to the hotel. That night, we have to go back to Iquique.

My dad says he needs to sleep before driving. He lies down. I start flipping through channels. I think about the list, and I look at it. I search for a pen in my bag, check off two more words, and put it away. I go on flipping channels. I sleep, and I dream. My grandfather is in his house, lying on the floor. I dream that my dad and I come in and find him like that, on the floor, surrounded by cockroaches, black ones and white ones that fly above his body. I go over to him and my dad leaves; he leaves me alone with my grandpa. My grandpa is talking; my grandpa says that my uncle isn't going to come back to life. He says this without opening his mouth, and the cockroaches go on flying over his body.

I open my eyes.

My dad is packing his bag. I get up and do the same. I put my tennis shoes next to the underwear. I ask him if he's talked to my grandpa. He says he hasn't. I tell him he should call him. "Later," he says, "we're running late." He asks if I'm hungry, and I say I am. He offers to take me out to a chicken joint called Pollo Pechugón. I remind him that the dentist said I couldn't eat anything solid. "It doesn't matter," he says, "we'll figure something out." We clear out the room, leave the bags in the truck, and walk to the restaurant. I avoid opening my mouth. I still taste blood. We go in, and my dad orders chicken with french fries. I order juice. I watch him eat. He asks me if I've enjoyed Tacna. I say yes, although I'm not so sure. He goes on eating. He offers me french fries. I accept a few. I have to take them and stuff them almost whole into my mouth. Chew with the molars in the back. The fries taste like blood. Like blood and the paste on my teeth. My dad eats chicken with french fries, no problem. He asks if the food is good. I look and him and say, "Yes, it's very good."

We walk toward the hotel. I have no idea what the street is called, but there are several casinos on it. Some Chileans are walking beside us, talking loudly. "This looks just like Chile," says one of them, as if it were the most important reflection of his life. My dad is looking at some receipts as he walks. I look at my list. Three items checked off. The rest, the majority, untouched. The Chileans speed up. We go into the hotel, head to the parking lot. My dad puts the receipts into a bag and gets into the truck. "Are you happy with the things you got, kiddo?" he asks. "Where did you put them?"

He starts the car. I tell him they're in my bag.

"That stuff'll get you through the year, right?"

We leave the hotel. Before we head to the border, he asks if I'd like to drive around Tacna a bit. I say O.K. I have to show him the list, I tell myself. I don't know how to bring it up. As he drives, he tells me the names of neighborhoods in Tacna. I want to tell him about the list. I want to ask him about my Uncle Neno. I want to tell him what happened with my mom. Now he's talking to me about cars; he says the Peruvians don't know how to buy cars, that they've got no class. He says that, and I think about his BMW 850i. His Honda Accord. I think about my Uncle Neno. About the list. He goes on talking about the Peruvians' bad taste, about the lack of stoplights in the city. The lack of streetlights. I take the list out of my bag and put it on my lap.

Now he's talking to me about Peruvian highways, about the way Peruvians drive. We're headed for the border. We're leaving the city behind. The radio isn't picking up any channels. There are no people. In the desert, there are no people. No dragons either. Everything is dark. Very dark. A collision. A crack. My dad has no time to brake. The lump in the middle of the highway. There's a crack in the windshield. My dad looks at me, puts his hand on my thigh, and tells me to stay calm. He puts the car in reverse. He turns the wheel, goes around it, and speeds up. We can see the lights at the border. I don't know where the list went.

For the rest of the trip we hardly speak at all. It's late. We cross the desert amid shadows and fog. I put my face up close to the window. I can see my reflection. My dad's. I try to look at the stars, but I can't see anything. "It's the desert fog, the camanchaca," says my dad. I look at him from the corner of my eye. He's driving over eighty-five miles an hour. I close my eyes. And I see them there, lying on the highway. The bodies. Children and old people, lying on the highway. I see them in the middle of the desert, and my dad drives around them. He speeds up and drives around.

LITERATURE
is not the same thing as
PUBLISHING

Coffee House Press began as a small letterpress operation in 1972 and has grown into an internationally renowned nonprofit publisher of literary fiction, essay, poetry, and other work that doesn't fit neatly into genre categories.

Coffee House is both a publisher and an arts organization. Through our *Books in Action* program and publications, we've become interdisciplinary collaborators and incubators for new work and audience experiences. Our vision for the future is one where a publisher is a catalyst and connector.

Funder Acknowledgments

Coffee House Press is an internationally renowned independent book publisher and arts nonprofit based in Minneapolis, MN; through its literary publications and *Books in Action* program, Coffee House acts as a catalyst and connector—between authors and readers, ideas and resources, creativity and community, inspiration and action.

Coffee House Press books are made possible through the generous support of grants and donations from corporations, state and federal grant programs, family foundations, and the many individuals who believe in the transformational power of literature. This activity is made possible by the voters of Minnesota through a Minnesota State Arts Board Operating Support grant, thanks to the legislative appropriation from the arts and cultural heritage fund. Coffee House also receives major operating support from the Amazon Literary Partnership, the Bush Foundation, the Jerome Foundation, The McKnight Foundation, Target Foundation, and the National Endowment for the Arts (NEA). To find out more about how NEA grants impact individuals and communities, visit www.arts.gov.

Coffee House Press receives additional support from the Elmer L. & Eleanor J. Andersen Foundation; the David & Mary Anderson Family Foundation; the Buuck Family Foundation; the Carolyn Foundation; the Dorsey & Whitney Foundation; Dorsey & Whitney LLP; the Knight Foundation; the Rehael Fund of the Minneapolis Foundation; the Matching Grant Program Fund of the Minneapolis Foundation; the Schwab Charitable Fund; Schwegman, Lundberg & Woessner, P.A.; the Scott Family Foundation; the US Bank Foundation; VSA Minnesota for the Metropolitan Regional Arts Council; the Archie D. & Bertha H. Walker Foundation; and the Woessner Freeman Family Foundation in honor of Allan Kornblum.

The Publisher's Circle of Coffee House Press

Publisher's Circle members make significant contributions to Coffee House Press's annual giving campaign. Understanding that a strong financial base is necessary for the press to meet the challenges and opportunities that arise each year, this group plays a crucial part in the success of Coffee House's mission.

Recent Publisher's Circle members include many anonymous donors, Mr. & Mrs. Rand L. Alexander, Suzanne Allen, Patricia A. Beithon, Bill Berkson & Connie Lewallen, the E. Thomas Binger & Rebecca Rand Fund of the Minneapolis Foundation, Robert & Gail Buuck, Claire Casey, Louise Copeland, Jane Dalrymple-Hollo, Ruth Stricker Dayton, Jennifer Kwon Dobbs & Stefan Liess, Mary Ebert & Paul Stembler, Chris Fischbach & Katie Dublinski, Kaywin Feldman & Jim Lutz, Sally French, Jocelyn Hale & Glenn Miller, the Rehael Fund-Roger Hale/Nor Hall of the Minneapolis Foundation, Randy Hartten & Ron Lotz, Jeffrey Hom, Carl & Heidi Horsch, Amy L. Hubbard & Geoffrey J. Kehoe Fund, Kenneth Kahn & Susan Dicker, Stephen & Isabel Keating, Kenneth Koch Literary Estate, Jennifer Komar & Enrique Olivarez, Allan & Cinda Kornblum, Leslie Larson Maheras, Lenfestey Family Foundation, Sarah Lutman & Rob Rudolph, the Carol & Aaron Mack Charitable Fund of the Minneapolis Foundation, George & Olga Mack, Joshua Mack, Gillian McCain, Mary & Malcolm McDermid, Sjur Midness & Briar Andresen, Maureen Millea Smith & Daniel Smith, Peter Nelson & Jennifer Swenson, Marc Porter & James Hennessy, Jeffrey Scherer, Jeffrey Sugerman & Sarah Schultz, Nan G. & Stephen C. Swid, Patricia Tilton, Stu Wilson & Melissa Barker, Warren D. Woessner & Iris C. Freeman, Margaret Wurtele, Joanne Von Blon, and Wayne P. Zink.

For more information about the Publisher's Circle and other ways to support Coffee House Press books, authors, and activities, please visit www.coffeehousepress.org/support or contact us at info@coffeehousepress.org.

Latin American Translation
from Coffee House Press

Among Strange Victims
by Daniel Saldaña París
Translated by Christina MacSweeney

Faces in the Crowd
by Valeria Luiselli
Translated by Christina MacSweeney

Sidewalks
by Valeria Luiselli
Translated by Christina MacSweeney

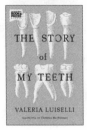

The Story of My Teeth
by Valeria Luiselli
Translated by Christina MacSweeney

DIEGO ZÚÑIGA is a Chilean author and journalist. He is the author of two novels and the recipient of the Juegos Literarios Gabriela Mistral Prize and the Chilean National Book and Reading Council Award. He lives in Santiago, Chile.

MEGAN McDOWELL is a Spanish-language literary translator whose work includes books by Alejandro Zambra, Arturo Fontaine, Lina Meruane, Mariana Enríquez, Álvaro Bisama, and Juan Emar. She lives in Santiago, Chile.

Camanchaca was designed by
Bookmobile Design & Digital Publisher Services.
Text is set in Adobe Garamond Pro.